© 2013 Disney Enterprises, Inc
Published by Hachette Partworks Ltd.
ISBN: 978-1-908648-95-2
Date of Printing: November 2013
Printed in Malaysia by Tien Wah Press
Based on the "Winnie the Pooh" works by
A.A. Milne and E.H. Shepard. All rights reserved.

Disney
Winnie the Pooh
and the Honey Tree

Disney

H hachette

One summer morning, deep in the Hundred-Acre Wood, Winnie the Pooh was doing his morning exercises when he heard his tummy rumble.

"Time for something sweet!" he declared.

Pooh looked in the cupboard, but all his honey pots were empty!

Then Pooh spotted a buzzy bee outside his window. Pooh knew that wherever there are bees, there is honey – so he followed the bee.

The bee disappeared
into a hole in a tree. Pooh
climbed up and poked his
paw into the hole. But the
bees did not want to share
with a bear. They swarmed
angrily round Pooh…

... until he lost his balance and fell off the branch, landing right in the middle of a prickly bush! "Oh bother," said Pooh, rubbing his head.

Just then, Christopher Robin came by,
holding a balloon.

"May I borrow your balloon?" asked Pooh.

Pooh had a plan. First of all, he rolled in a
muddy puddle, then he took hold of the balloon.

"I'll fly up into the honey-bee tree!" Pooh
explained.

"My disguise will make the
bees think I'm a little black rain
cloud," he added.

"Silly old bear," said
Christopher Robin. "Good luck!"

Pooh just managed to swipe
a pawful of golden honey
before he was surrounded by
bees. They weren't fooled by
Pooh's disguise!

Suddenly, the balloon began to lose air. It zoomed away, taking Pooh with it!

"Oh my! Help!" cried Pooh, as the balloon zoomed towards the ground – and Christopher Robin!

Luckily, Pooh landed in Christopher Robin's lap. "I don't think I look very much like a little black rain cloud," decided Pooh.

"I'm still hungry," said Pooh. "I wonder if my good friend Rabbit has any honey?"

So Pooh went to Rabbit's house to remind him it was lunchtime.

"What would you like in your sandwich?" Rabbit asked Pooh.

"I'd like a honey sandwich, please," replied Pooh. "But without the bread."

Pooh ate and ate, then he ate some more. And then he ate even more!

"Have you finished?" asked Rabbit grumpily.

"Yes, and I'd better be going," said Pooh, rubbing his very full tummy. "Goodbye, Rabbit."

Pooh started out of the door, but halfway through, his tummy got stuck!

"Oh bother!" said Pooh.

Rabbit pushed and pulled and
shoved and tugged, but Pooh
stayed stuck.

So Rabbit went out through his
back door to see if he could free
Pooh from outside.

But Pooh still wouldn't budge.

"It's no use," said Rabbit. "I'll go and get
Christopher Robin."

"Cheer up, Pooh," said Christopher
Robin. "We'll get you out."
With Rabbit and Owl's help, Christopher
Robin grabbed and dragged and
pressed and pushed.

But Pooh didn't budge an inch.
"We'll just have to wait until you get thin again," said Christopher Robin.

"How long will that take?" asked Pooh.
"Who knows?" said Owl.

Day after day and night after night, everyone waited for Pooh to get thin. To cheer him up, Christopher Robin read him stories and Owl tried to teach him long words.

Kanga and Roo brought Pooh a blue
scarf to keep him warm while he waited
to get thinner.

Even Eeyore visited and tried to make
his friend feel better.

Then one morning, when Rabbit pushed
against Pooh, he felt the bear move a little!
    Rabbit raced off to get Christopher Robin
and the others.

Everybody pulled from the outside, while Rabbit
pushed from the inside until, all of a sudden, Pooh
shot out and flew through the air…

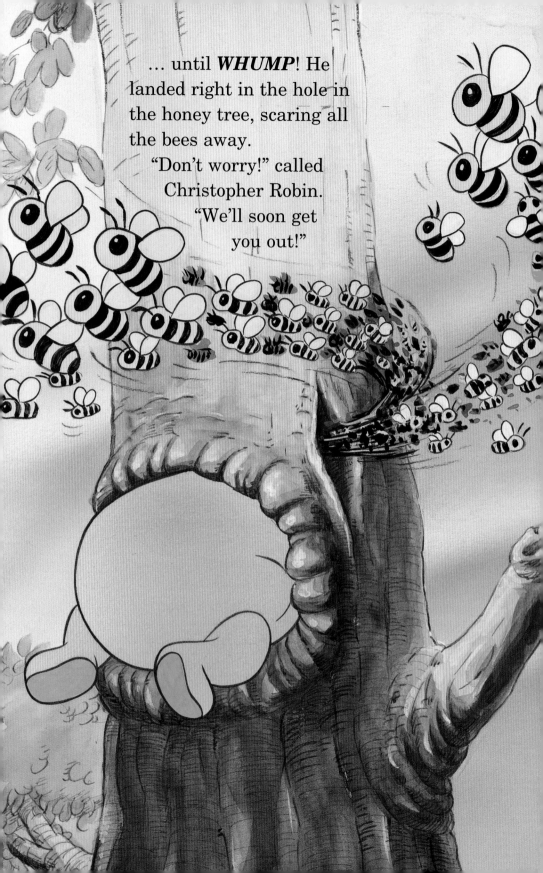

… until **WHUMP**! He landed right in the hole in the honey tree, scaring all the bees away.

"Don't worry!" called Christopher Robin. "We'll soon get you out!"

A muffled sound came from inside the tree. "Oh, no hurry," replied Pooh with his mouth full. "Take all the time you need..."

Nise For Piknics

Piglet

Rabbit e
Howse

Sandpit where
Roo plays

Owl

Pooh Bears Howse

100 Aker Wood

Floody Place